Cows
can't
Fly

For Bill
and
Steve

Houghton Mifflin Edition, 2001

Printed in the U.S.A.

ISBN: 0-618-06706-X

123456789-B-06 05 04 03 02 01 00

Cows
Can't
Fly

Written and Illustrated
by David Milgrim

 HOUGHTON MIFFLIN   BOSTON • MORRIS PLAINS, NJ

California • Colorado • Georgia • Illinois • New Jersey • Texas

Cows can't fly,
but I don't care.

One day I drew
some in the air!

"Why, that's absurd,"
my father said.
"Why don't you draw
some birds instead?"

But then, like magic,
came a breeze
that grabbed my cows
and shook the trees.

And in a breath,
before my eyes,

my flying cows
were flying high!

My drawing flew off
far away,

but where it went
I cannot say. . . .

Next thing I knew,
to my surprise,

a flock of cattle
fluttered by!

They flapped and flew
and filled the sky,

quite unaware
that cows can't fly.

I ran inside
and told my dad,
but he thought I
was raving mad.

"I'd love to see
a flying cow,"
my mother said,
"but not just now."

My grandma said,
"If cows can fly,

then why, pray tell,
can't you and I?"

Ms. Crumb said cows
were far too fat;

that facts were facts,
and that was that.

And everyone
I told downtown

was much too busy
looking down.

So no one saw
the cows but me,

but what a sight
they were to see!

And when they left,
I grabbed my pen

and sat right down
to draw again.

Because if cows
can soar the sky,

who knows what else
might start to fly. . . .